FIRST SCIENCE EXPERIMENTS

EXPERIMENTS
WITH
FORCES

By Anna Claybourne

WINDMILL
BOOKS

Published in 2017 by **Windmill Books**, an Imprint of Rosen Publishing
29 East 21st Street, New York, NY 10010

Author: Anna Claybourne
Designer: Emma Randall
Illustrations: Caroline Romanet

CATALOGING-IN-PUBLICATION DATA

Names: Claybourne, Anna.
Title: Experiments with forces / Anna Claybourne.
Description: New York : Windmill Books, 2017. | Series: First science experiments |
    Includes index.
Identifiers: ISBN 9781508192428 (pbk.) | ISBN 9781508192381 (library bound) |
    ISBN 9781508192305 (6 pack)
Subjects: LCSH: Force and energy--Experiments--Juvenile literature. |
    Science--Experiments--Juvenile literature.
Classification: LCC QC73.4 C627 2017 | DDC 531'.6--dc23

Manufactured in the United States of America
CPSIA Compliance Information: Batch #BS16PK: For Further Information contact Rosen Publishing, New York, New York at 1-800-237-9932

Contents

Introduction

Science means finding out about the world, and all the stuff in it. That's why scientists do experiments – to find out as much as they can!

Science tips

· Clear a neat, empty space for doing experiments in.
· Check if it's OK to use the things in the "You will need" boxes with whoever owns them!
· For messy experiments, wear old clothes, not your best outfit!
· Do messy experiments outdoors, if you can.
· Remember to clean up the mess afterwards!

GET AN ADULT ASSISTANT

For some of the experiments, you'll need to heat things, cook things, chop things up, or use electrical items. For anything like this, make sure you have an adult handy to help you.

KEEPING RECORDS

Real scientists don't just do experiments - they also keep records. To do this, you could take photos of your experiments or draw pictures of them, and write down what happened.

Try it yourself!

This book is full of easy but exciting experiments for you to try for yourself. For most of them, you only need a few basic things that you can find at home.

Are you ready to experiment? Turn the page and let's get started!

Forces

How do you make a tower of bricks fall over? Push it! How do you get a toboggan up a hill? Pull it! These pushes and pulls are called forces. They are everywhere, making things around us move, stop, or change shape.

PUSH

A push can make something move, like when you push a scooter along with your foot. Pushes can also make things fall over, or get squashed - like when you squeeze putty.

PULL

A pull can make something move, like when you pull a plug out of a drain. It can also make something stretch, like a rubber band.

Working together

There is often more than one force at work at the same time. The push of the bat makes a ball fly forward. At the same time, gravity pulls it down.

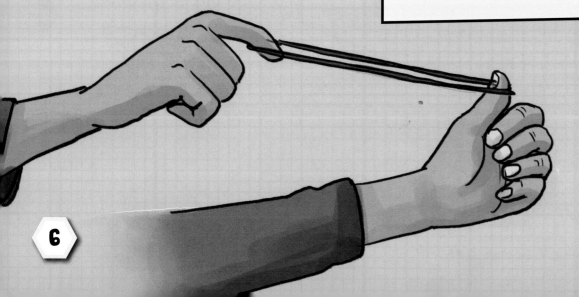

GRAVITY

Gravity is a pulling force between objects. The Earth is a huge object, and has lots of gravity. So when you jump up, the Earth's gravity pulls you down again.

FRICTION

Friction is a dragging force. It makes things slow down or grip when they rub on each other. Bike brakes use friction to slow down wheels. Sneaker soles use friction to grip the ground.

Try this!

Take two toy cars, and zoom them towards each other at high speed. Your hand pushes a car and makes it move.

The cars stop when they push against each other. The cars may fly up in the air, then gravity pulls them down.

Balloon rocket

What makes a rocket blast off into space? Rockets push gases out of their engines. The gas pushes back, and this makes the rocket move. Make this model balloon rocket to see how it works.

1 Cut a piece of string 10-13 feet (3-4 m) long. Thread the straw onto it.

2 Ask two people to hold the ends of the string and pull it tight. (Or you could tie it to something.)

3

Blow up the balloon but don't knot it shut - just hold it firmly closed.

4

While you hold it, ask someone to tape the balloon to the straw, like this.

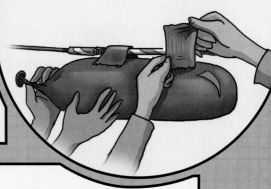

5

Move the balloon and straw along to the end of the string, with the open end of the balloon pointing back.

Try this!

Can you make the balloon move uphill along a sloping string? Or does it have to be flat?

6

Ready, steady... let go of the balloon! It should ZOOM along the string!

Another fun idea

Can you make two teams, each with their own balloon rocket, and have a race?

What has happened?

When you let go, the air comes rushing out of the balloon. As it moves, it pushes back against the balloon. The pushing force makes the balloon move along the string. Real rockets work the same way.

Marble run

A marble can roll all the way through a maze by itself – as long as the force of gravity is pulling it. Make your own marble run and watch the marbles roll down to the end!

You will need:

- Marbles
- Several cardboard tubes from rolls of paper towel or toilet paper
- Scissors
- A fridge or cupboard door, or other upright surface that you can put adhesive tape on.

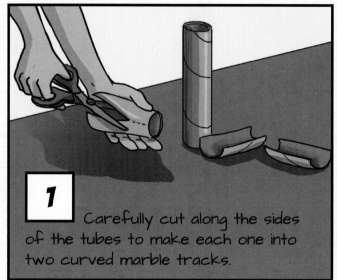

1 Carefully cut along the sides of the tubes to make each one into two curved marble tracks.

2 Start making a path for your marbles by taping the tracks to your upright surface.

Another fun idea
Can you make a 3-D, free-standing marble run? Use whole cardboard tubes as towers, and see if you can link them together.

3

Tape along the side of each track, then add a bit more tape over the top to make it stronger.

4

Each track must slope downhill, and lead to another track. Use as many as you can to make a path for the marbles from top to bottom. When it's ready, hold a marble at the starting point, and let it roll!

5

Can you time how long your marble takes? Does it speed up as it goes?

What has happened?

The Earth's gravity pulls down on things all the time. If there is a flat surface in the way, it stops them from falling. But if the surface is sloped, objects can get pulled down the slope, towards the Earth. Balls, such as marbles, move downhill very easily, because they roll, instead of sliding.

Balancing shapes

If you spread your arms out, you can balance on one tiptoe – for a little while! But soon, you topple over. Balancing depends on how gravity pulls on objects. Try balancing these shapes, and you might be amazed!

You will need:

- Tracing paper
- Pens
- Card stock
- Scissors
- Small coins
- Adhesive tape
- Thin string

BALANCING BUTTERFLY

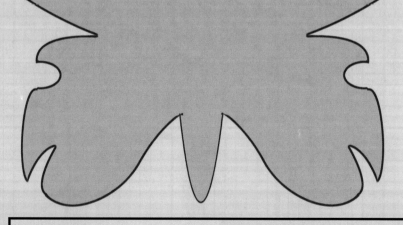

1 Trace this butterfly, cut it out, and draw around it onto a piece of card stock.

2 Cut out your butterfly (you can also color it in if you like). Tape two coins under the front wingtips.

3 You should now be able to balance the butterfly on your fingertip, by the tip of its nose.

TIGHTROPE CLOWN

1 Trace the clown, cut it out, and draw around it onto a piece of card stock.

2 Cut out and decorate your clown. Tape two coins under his hands.

Try this!
How far can you lean to one side without falling over? Not far. The center of gravity of a human is quite high up, somewhere in your stomach. If your feet are directly under your center of gravity, you stay up, but if you lean sideways so that your feet aren't under it, you start to topple.

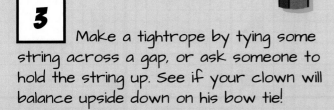

3 Make a tightrope by tying some string across a gap, or ask someone to hold the string up. See if your clown will balance upside down on his bow tie!

What has happened?

Objects balance because they have a "center of gravity". The object's weight is spread out evenly around this point. If the object rests on a point in line with its center of gravity, it balances. You would expect these shapes to fall, but the coins move their center of gravity, making them balance.

Spoon shooter

Have you ever tried to throw an apple core in the trash, or taken a shot at a basketball hoop? You have to get it just right!

You will need:

- A long wooden or metal spoon
- A ruler
- Rubber bands
- Balled-up pairs of socks
- Scrunched-up paper balls
- A plastic bowl

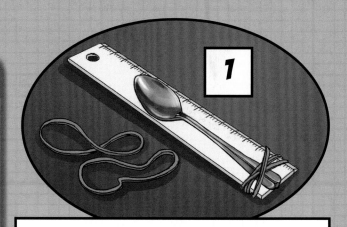

1

Lay the spoon on top of the ruler, with the ends of the ruler and the spoon handle lining up. Loop several rubber bands tightly around the handle end to hold them firmly together.

2 Stuff one or two pairs of socks between the spoon and the ruler, close to the rubber bands. This will make the curved end of the spoon stick up.

3 Put the plastic bowl a short distance away as a target to shoot at. Make some scrunched-up paper cannonballs.

4 Holding the ruler still, gently push down the bowl end of the spoon, and sit a cannonball in it.

5 To shoot the cannonball, let the spoon go so that it flips back up. Fire!

Another fun idea
What else will your spoon shooter shoot? Try ping-pong balls, marshmallows or raisins (but you might want to avoid anything too hard or messy!).

What has happened?
As the spoon flips back up, it pushes your cannonball into the air. Friction with the air slows the ball down. As it slows, gravity pulls it to the ground. This creates a smooth, curved path through the air. When you aim, you have to balance your pushing force with the way friction and gravity will work, to get that curve exactly right When you do – PLOP! A hole in one!

Magic magazines!

How hard can a magazine hold on? You're about to find out!

1 Lie the magazines down next to each other and open them up.

2 Lie the front page of one magazine over the back page of the other. Then fold down a page from the first magazine, then a page from the other, and so on.

3 Keep interleaving the pages of the magazines until they are all used up. Press the magazines tightly closed.

4 Try to pull the magazines apart. Why is it so hard?!?

What has happened?

The rough paper pages have a lot of friction – a dragging, gripping force. When they rub against each other, they grip and hold tight. You could easily pull two or four pages apart. But when all the pages are together, there's so much friction that they hold on very tightly.

Eraser slide

Friction helps things grip – but what if you don't want that? This experiment shows you how you can make less friction.

1 Make a gentle slope by propping the tray up on the box. Try sliding some erasers down it.

2 Erasers have good friction, and it's hard to make them slide. Take them off, and dribble some oil over your tray slide.

3 Now try again. Do the erasers slide more easily?

Another fun idea
Try holding a plastic bottle full of water with dry hands, wet hands, and oily hands.

What has happened?

The erasers and the tray grip each other as they rub together. When you add a layer of liquid oil, it flows in between them and separates them. That makes it much harder for them to grip.

17

Does water have skin?

Pins and needles are made of metal. Drop them in water, and they'll sink. But if you are very careful, you can make them sit on the water surface. It's as if a "skin" holds them up.

You will need:

- Coins, pins and needles, and paper clips or small safety pins
- A large bowl of water
- Paper towels

ON THE WATER

1 Let the water in your bowl settle until it is still. Drop in a pin or needle, pointing downwards. What happens?

2 Now try gently laying a pin or needle flat on the surface. If it's tricky, try using a bit of paper towel to put it on.

THE BULGING COIN

1 Put down a coin on the tabletop.

Another fun idea

Here's a twist on experiment with pins or needles on the opposite page. Try adding a drop of liquid soap to water... and the pins will sink! Soap breaks up surface tension, stopping it from working for a while.

2 **3** Carefully add more and more drops onto the coin. What happens? How many drops can you add?

Dip your finger in your bowl of water, and start dripping drops of water onto the coin.

What has happened?

Water does not actually have a skin. But water molecules – the tiny bits that make up water – have a pulling force. They pull together extra hard on the surface. This is called surface tension, and it makes the water surface harder to break. This gives it a "skin" that objects can rest on. It also pulls the water on the coin together, so it can pile up in a big bulge.

Diving bell

Before submarines and scuba gear, people could go underwater using a diving bell. They could even breathe underwater. How did it work?

1 Tear a small strip off the paper tissue. Wrap it around the toy figure like a bandage and use the rubber band or thread to hold it on.

2 Put the toy inside the glass. Use a blob of plasticine or sticky tack to stick its head to the base of the glass.

3

Turn the glass upside down, with the toy figure inside. Carefully push it down into the water until the glass touches the bottom.

4

Can you see what's happening inside the glass? Is it filling up with water?

Try this!

Try the experiment again, but while the glass is underwater, slowly turn it the right way up. What happens?

5

Keeping the glass upside down, carefully lift it out. Dry your hands and remove the toy. If it has stayed dry, the paper tissue will not be damp.

What has happened?

You can't see air, but it takes up space and has a pushing force, called air pressure. The air trapped inside the glass pushes down, so water cannot get in. The toy stays dry inside. If it were alive, it would be able to breathe the air for a while too. People used to go underwater in much bigger diving bells.

Bottle ball

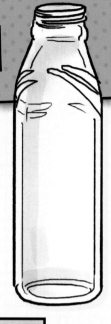

It should be easy to blow a paper ball into a bottle, right? Wrong!

1 Lie the bottle down flat on a table. Gently put the paper ball just inside the bottle neck.

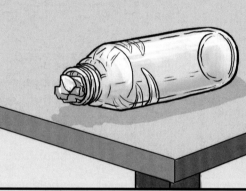

Try this!
Can you make the ball go into the bottle by sucking air out of the bottle with a straw?

2 Challenge a friend to blow the ball into the bottle - or try doing it yourself! It's impossible.

What has happened?

The bottle has no liquid in it, but it's not empty – it's full of air. When you blow into it, you add even more air. The air pushes its way back out of the bottle, and pushes the ball out too.

The stuck ruler

You will need:

- A flat wooden, metal or plastic 12-inch (30 cm) ruler
- A large sheet of newspaper
- A table

A sheet of newspaper doesn't weigh much. So it should be easy to lift up. But with this experiment, it's harder than it looks!

1 Lie the ruler down so that it is sticking out over the edge of the table.

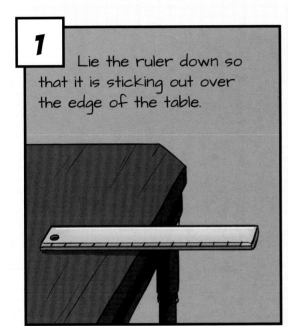

2 Spread the sheet of newspaper out over the ruler and smooth it down flat.

3 Now smack your hand down hard on the end of the ruler. You might expect it to push the paper up. What actually happens?

What has happened?

The paper has very little air underneath it, but lots of air on top. The air pressure from all this air pushes down on the paper, and holds the ruler down too.

The speed of gravity

How fast does gravity pull things down?
Does it depend on how heavy they are?

You will need:

- A feather
- A coin or marble
- Two matching plastic or cardboard containers with lids

1 Check if the coin or marble feels heavier than the feather - it should be. If you have digital cooking scales, you could weigh them both.

2 Put the coin or marble in one hand and the feather in the other, and hold them out in front of you.

Try this!
If you have a video camera or camera phone, you could ask someone to video the objects as you drop them. Then watch the video in slow motion, to get a really good look.

3 Drop the coin or marble and the feather, making sure you let go of them at exactly the same time. Which hits the ground first?

4 Now put the coin or marble inside one container, and the feather inside the other, and close the lids.

Check that the container with the marble inside is still heavier than the one with the feather inside.

5 Hold out both containers, and drop them at exactly the same time, as before. Now which one hits the ground first?

What has happened?

When the objects are not inside the containers, the feather falls more slowly – but when they are, they fall at the same speed. Gravity pulls lighter and heavier objects at the same speed. However, in air, a light, fluffy object like a feather will get slowed down more by the air in its way. This is called air resistance, and is a type of force.

Fun with magnets

Magnets have a special kind of force, called magnetism. They can pull some metal objects towards them, as if by magic.

You will need:

- One or more strong magnets
- Metal paper clips
- String
- Adhesive tape
- Thin card stock
- Colored pens

ANTI-GRAVITY PAPER CLIPS

1 Tie several paper clips to short lengths of string. Tape the other ends of the strings to a table or the floor.

2 Use a magnet to get the paper clips to reach up into the air, pulling on their strings. Can you make them move?

Try this!

If you have two magnets, try letting them pull towards each other. Then turn one around, and see if you can feel the magnets pushing apart. They do this when the matching ends of the magnets are near each other.

STRING OF CLIPS

Hold a magnet up and put a paper clip close to it, so that it clings on.

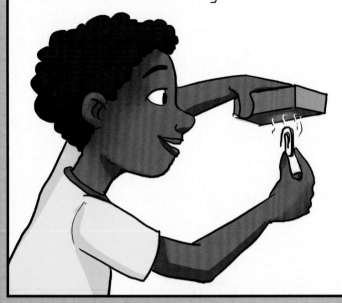

Hold another paper clip near that paper clip, and see if it will cling on. Add another, and another. How long can you make your string of clips?

MAGIC MAZE

1

Draw a maze on your piece of card stock. Then put a paper clip on top of the card stock, and your magnet underneath.

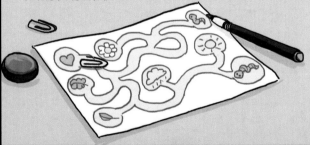

2

Can you use the magnet to make the clip move through the maze?

What has happened?

Magnets can pull on some types of metal, and on other magnets. When a metal object, like a paper clip, is touching a magnet, it becomes a magnet too. Magnetism is invisible, and it can work across empty space and through other things, like card stock.

Jet planes like these fly by pushing gas out behind them, like the balloon rocket in this book. Planes have engines that burn fuel to make the gas. As the gas pushes back, the plane gets pushed forward - at enormous speed!

A parachutist can jump out of a plane and fall slowly, instead of plummeting to the ground. The parachute provides lots of air resistance, slowing their fall.

Take a close look at a pond, and you might see insects like these pond skaters on the surface. They skate to and fro, using the water's surface tension to hold them up.

On a normal day, rubber-soled sneakers grip the ground. The friction means you can't slide far. On ice, though, you can slide a long way. The ice has a thin layer of water on the surface, which reduces friction.

Further information

Books

All About Forces by Angela Royston (Heinemann Educational Books, 2016)

Mind Webs: Forces and Motion by Anna Claybourne (Wayland, 2014)

Moving Up with Science: Forces and Magnets by Peter Riley (Franklin Watts, 2016)

Ride that Rollercoaster!: Forces at an Amusement Park by Richard and Louise Spilsbury (Heinemann Educational Books, 2015)

Websites

For web resources related to the subject of this book, go to: **www.windmillbooks.com/weblinks** and select this book's title.

Glossary

air pressure
The force of air as it pushes on things.

air resistance
A type of friction that slows an object's movement through the air.

balance
Holding a position by having the same weight on either side.

center of gravity
The point that marks the center of an object's weight, so that it acts as a balancing point.

friction
A force that slows moving objects.

gas
A substance that is like air and has no fixed shape.

gravity
A natural force that pulls objects toward each other, such as the force that causes things to fall toward the Earth.

interleaving
Putting something between the pages of a book.

magnet
An object that is able to pull some types of metal toward it.

magnetism
A way that a material pulls or pushes away another material.

surface tension
A force of resistance felt on the surface of a liquid.

water molecules
The smallest unit of water that is still water.

Index